The Tooth Fairy Went Broke

The Tooth Fairy Went Broke

The Tooth Fairy Went Broke

The Tooth Fairy Went Broke

The Tooth Fairy Went Broke

The Tooth Fairy Went Broke

The Tooth Fairy Went Broke

The Tooth Fairy Went Broke

The Tooth Fairy Went Broke

The Tooth Fairy Went Broke

To order additional copies of this book, contact:
Xlibris
1-888-795-4274
www.Xlibris.com
Orders@Xlibris.com

ISBN: 978-1-9845-7897-6 (sc)
ISBN: 978-1-9845-7898-3 (e)

Print information available on the last page

Rev. date: 07/17/2020

The Tooth Fairy Went Broke

The Tooth Fairy Went Broke

The Tooth Fairy Went Broke

The Tooth Fairy Went Broke

The Tooth Fairy Went Broke

The Tooth Fairy Went Broke

The Tooth Fairy Went Broke

The Tooth Fairy Went Broke

The Tooth Fairy Went Broke

The Tooth Fairy Went Broke

The tooth fairy was always good at leaving money under the pillows of little boys and girls who were anxious about losing a tooth.

The tooth fairy saw
all kinds of teeth.
She saw small teeth, big teeth,
clean teeth, dirty teeth, and
she even saw rotten teeth.

On one particular day, when
the tooth fairy went to
do her normal rounds, she
realized she had no money
left to give the children.

But that didn't stop the tooth fairy from doing her job.

Instead of money, she decided to leave special fairy treats that would reveal magical toy creatures as they were eaten by the children.

The tooth fairy was very happy
when she saw that little boys
and girls loved this change.

The tooth fairy left a
note thanking all the little
boys and girls for being
so understanding.

The Tooth Fairy Went Broke

The Tooth Fairy Went Broke

The Tooth Fairy Went Broke

The Tooth Fairy Went Broke

The Tooth Fairy Went Broke

The Tooth Fairy Went Broke

The Tooth Fairy Went Broke

The Tooth Fairy Went Broke

The Tooth Fairy Went Broke

The Tooth Fairy Went Broke

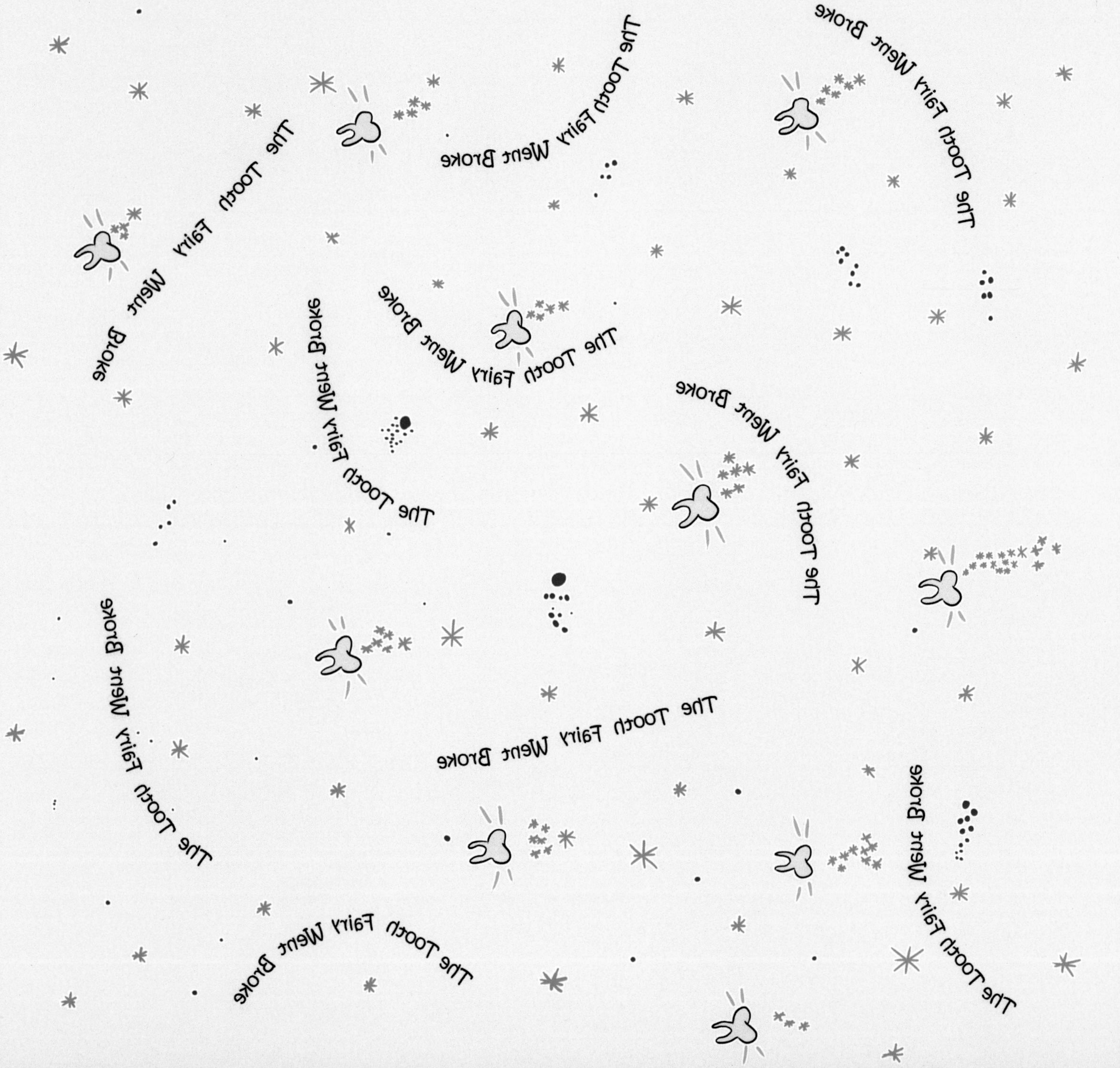

The Tooth Fairy Went Broke

The Tooth Fairy Went Broke

The Tooth Fairy Went Broke

The Tooth Fairy Went Broke

The Tooth Fairy Went Broke

The Tooth Fairy Went Broke

The Tooth Fairy Went Broke

The Tooth Fairy Went Broke

The Tooth Fairy Went Broke

The Tooth Fairy Went Broke

Printed in the United States
By Bookmasters